This
Ladybird book
belongs to

. . . .

For Mathew,
with llove
C.G.

For my family
M.H.

LADYBIRD BOOKS

UK | USA | Canada | Ireland | Australia | India | New Zealand | South Africa
Ladybird Books is part of the Penguin Random House group of companies
whose addresses can be found at global.penguinrandomhouse.com.
www.penguin.co.uk   www.puffin.co.uk   www.ladybird.co.uk

 Penguin
Random House
UK

First published 2019
001
Written by Charlie Green. Text copyright © Ladybird Books Ltd, 2019
Illustrations copyright © Matt Hunt, 2019
Moral rights asserted
Printed in Great Britain
A CIP catalogue record for this book is available from the British Library
ISBN: 978–0–241–39270–6
All correspondence to:
Ladybird Books, Penguin Random House Children's
80 Strand, London WC2R 0RL

CHOOSE LLAMAS!

Written by

Charlie Green

Illustrated by

Matt Hunt

Are you ready to build your very own llama squad?

This book is full of
a whole llotta llamas!

We are all different.

Each of us is amazing
in our own unique way.

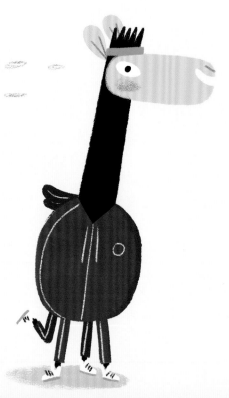

Which llamas do you feel drawn to?
There are no wrong answers.

But you
should definitely
pick me.

It's up to the reader, Colin!

It's time to CHOOSE.

Which llama would you choose to hang out with at the beach?

I love surfing!
What's **your** favourite
thing to do at
the seaside?

Jimbo

Frieda

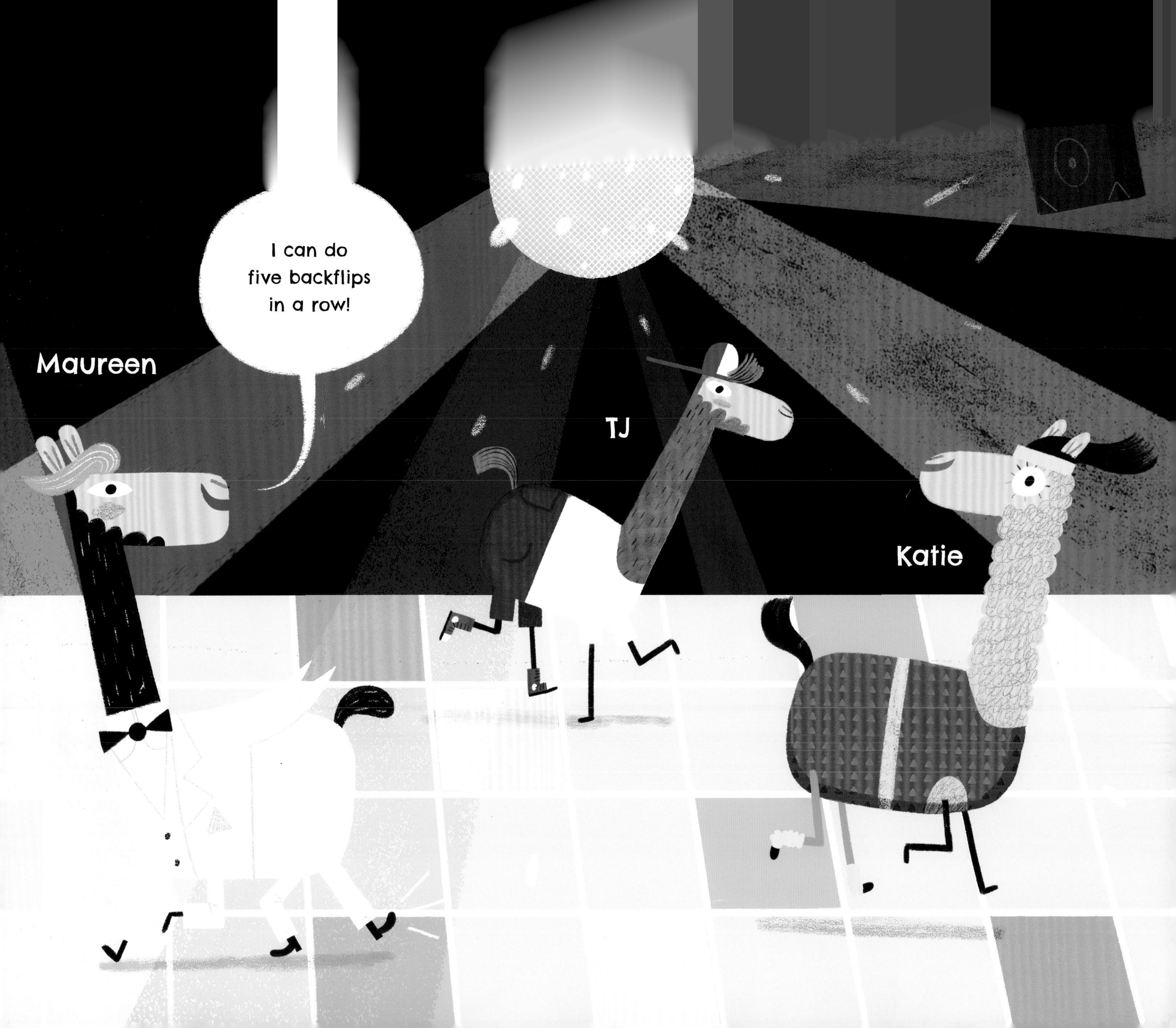
I can do five backflips in a row!
Maureen
TJ
Katie

Which llama would you choose to be your superhero sidekick?

I have super-llama strength! What would **your** superhero power be?

Lucas

Lydia

Mo

Which llama would you choose to go on safari with?

Is it lunchtime yet?

Neil

Jamila

Neil, it's ten o'clock
in the morning.
You've just had breakfast!

Here we are in
the African savanna.
Which wild animals
would **YOU** like to
see on safari?

Poppy

Gloria

David

Kendrick

THE LLAMAS

OK, let's rock!

Aisha

Ruby

Which llama would you choose to be your hairdresser?

What sort of haircut do **YOU** fancy today?

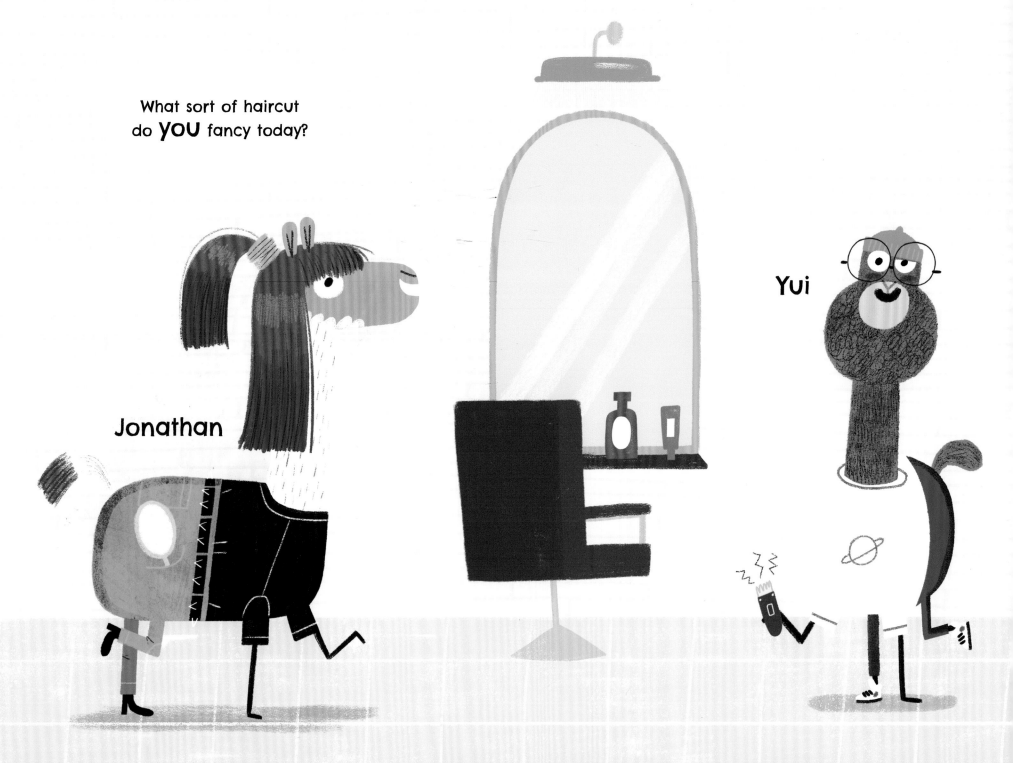

Jonathan

Yui

SHEAR  DELIGHT

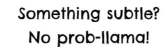

Something subtle?
No prob-llama!

1 2 3
4 5 6

Laura

Zoe

Francesco

Which llama would you choose to be your ice-skating partner?

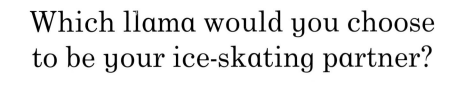

I love spinning around on the ice! Have **YOU** ever been ice skating?

I have a flawless combination of grace and agility.

Harry

Humphrey

Which llama would you choose to win this high-speed llama race?

Which llama would you choose to chill out with?

Llamas in pyjamas. No dramas. What else rhymes with 'llama'?

Megan

Elijah

Benjamin

THE LLAMAS

I am very relaxed!
Incredibly relaxed!
What was that?

Can someone pass
the ice cream, please?

Wilbur

LLAMAGEDDON
BRUCE WOOLIS

Shanaya

Which llama would you choose to fly to space with?

Valentina

Prisha

When I get nervous I have to stand upside down on my head.

Floyd
Which objects would YOU bring to space?
Selena
Theodore
I would bring
two things to space:
1. My space boots
2. Style

What a magnificent llama squad!
Just one question remains.

Who do the llamas choose
to be their best friend?

They choose
YOU!

Did you know . . . ?

Stephanie

Llamas are related to camels, but we don't have the hump!

That doesn't mean we don't get annoyed though . . . sometimes we stick out our tongues to show we are not impressed.

Olivia

Llamas can grow to 1.8 metres (6 feet) tall. That's the same height as you sitting on the back of a panda who is riding a baby unicorn. Promise.

Colin

Mother llamas hum to their babies. Sometimes we even take song requests.

We are very intelligent and curious creatures. Sorry, give me a minute – MI6 are calling.

Katie

Geoffrey

Baby llamas are called crias – pronounced *kree-uh* not *cry-uh*. Ah, babies make me come over all emotional.

Max

About 4,000 years ago, people in the place we now call Peru trained us to transport things on our backs. We can carry a quarter of our body weight . . .

. . . but if you overload us, we will simply lie down and refuse to move.

Megan

Lydia

Llamas' stomachs have three compartments. Boy, do we love to chomp.

We are herbivores. That means we always eat our greens!

Jamila

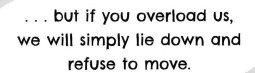

Yui

Our poo is a great fertiliser. We are 'communal defecators', which means we all like to poo in the same spot.

Evelyn

We can reach speeds of over 55 kilometres per hour (35 mph). Catch me if you can!

Matilda